A catalogue record for this book is available from the British Library

Published by Ladybird Books Ltd Loughborough Leicestershire UK
Ladybird Books Ltd is a subsidiary of the Penguin Group of companies
LADYBIRD and the device of a Ladybird are trademarks of Ladybird Books Ltd

Disney's

THE HUNCHBACK OF NOTRE DAME

Ladybird

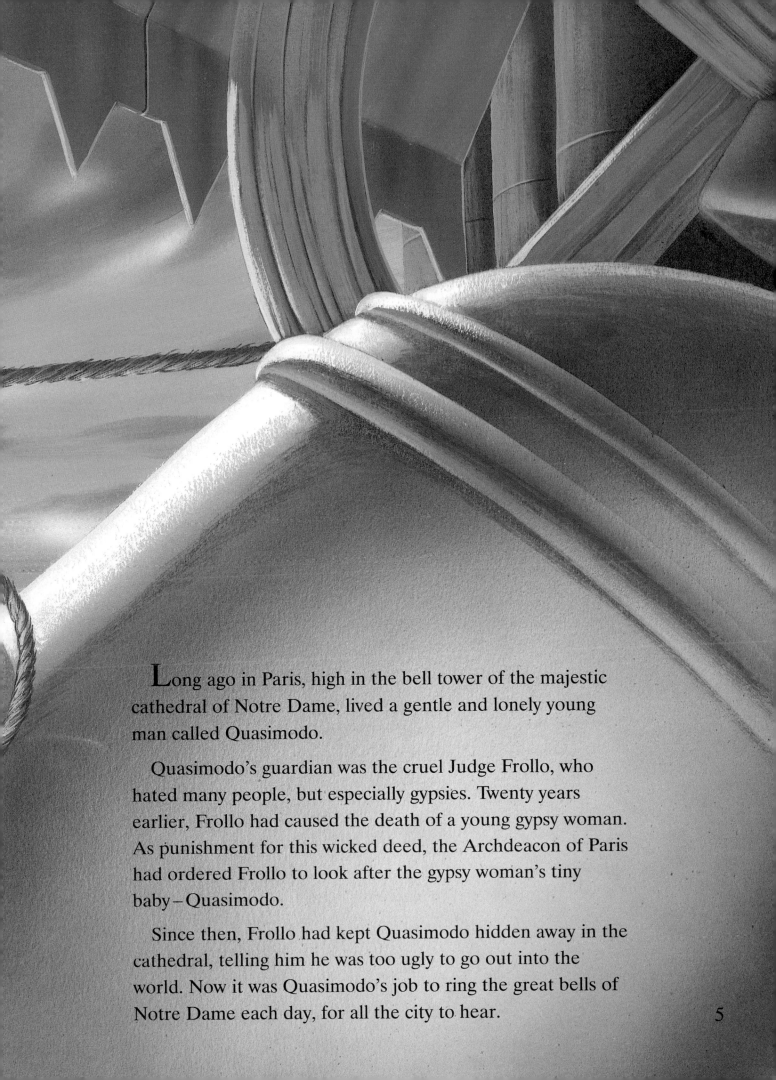

Long ago in Paris, high in the bell tower of the majestic cathedral of Notre Dame, lived a gentle and lonely young man called Quasimodo.

Quasimodo's guardian was the cruel Judge Frollo, who hated many people, but especially gypsies. Twenty years earlier, Frollo had caused the death of a young gypsy woman. As punishment for this wicked deed, the Archdeacon of Paris had ordered Frollo to look after the gypsy woman's tiny baby – Quasimodo.

Since then, Frollo had kept Quasimodo hidden away in the cathedral, telling him he was too ugly to go out into the world. Now it was Quasimodo's job to ring the great bells of Notre Dame each day, for all the city to hear.

5

Though Quasimodo lived alone, he had three faithful companions – Hugo, Laverne and Victor. To everyone else these creatures were just stone gargoyles. But to Quasimodo they were living, talking friends.

Today the gargoyles were looking forward to watching the most amazing festival of the year – the Festival of Fools – with Quasimodo. Every year the people of Paris enjoyed the topsy turvy fun of the day.

But Quasimodo was not in the mood for fun. He stayed inside, gazing sadly at the miniature model of Paris he had built in his room.

"**D**id you ever think of *going* to the festival?" Laverne asked Quasimodo.

"That's all I *ever* think about," Quasimodo replied. "But I'd never fit in out there. I'm not… normal."

The gargoyles weren't convinced. They insisted that Quasimodo should go to the festival, until at last he agreed.

Just then, Frollo arrived and discovered that Quasimodo was planning to attend the festival.

He quickly convinced Quasimodo that this was not a good idea, telling him that the townspeople would treat him like a monster. "Remember," said Frollo, "this cathedral is your sanctuary—the one place where you are safe."

In a nearby street, a beautiful gypsy called Esmeralda
played the tambourine while her little goat, Djali, danced.
Passers-by stopped to watch and drop coins into a hat.

In the crowd was the handsome Phoebus, who had just
arrived in Paris to be Frollo's new Captain of the Guard.
His eyes met Esmeralda's and for a moment they held each
other's gaze.

Suddenly, a gypsy signalled that trouble was near. Djali
grabbed the hat in his teeth, spilling all the coins. As Esmeralda
rushed to gather up the money, two soldiers approached.

Certain that she had stolen the money, the soldiers grabbed Esmeralda and took away the hat. Esmeralda struggled to get free and with a little help from Djali she finally managed to escape.

Phoebus, who had seen everything, commanded his horse to sit on one of the soldiers, giving Esmeralda and Djali enough time to disappear down an alley.

A short while later, Phoebus reported to Frollo at the Palace of Justice. As they stood on a balcony, Frollo glanced down at the street and saw Esmeralda dancing before an enthusiastic crowd.

"Look, Captain – gypsies," sneered Frollo. "I believe they have a safe haven in this very city which they call the Court of Miracles."

"And what are we going to do about it, Sir?" Phoebus asked.

In reply, Frollo viciously crushed a nest of ants he had found.

Phoebus began to have grave doubts about Frollo's idea of justice.

Meanwhile, the gargoyles had finally convinced Quasimodo to go to the festival, despite Frollo's warning. Disguised in a hooded robe, he swung down into the square.

The celebrations were well under way. People everywhere were dressed in funny costumes, singing and dancing and having fun. Quasimodo tried to keep out of sight but he couldn't avoid being swept up in the merrymaking.

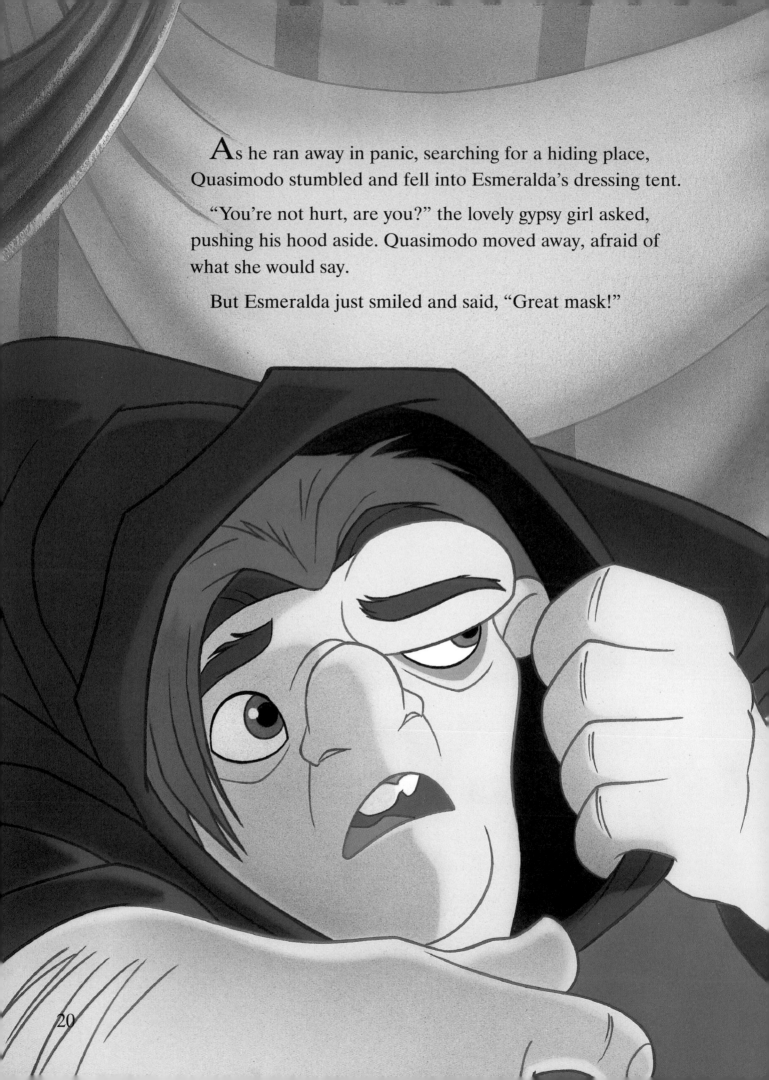

As he ran away in panic, searching for a hiding place, Quasimodo stumbled and fell into Esmeralda's dressing tent.

"You're not hurt, are you?" the lovely gypsy girl asked, pushing his hood aside. Quasimodo moved away, afraid of what she would say.

But Esmeralda just smiled and said, "Great mask!"

Realising that he didn't need a disguise, Quasimodo joined the festivities.

Soon it was time for Esmeralda to perform. As she danced next to Quasimodo, Esmeralda winked at him, making him blush.

When Esmeralda's dance was finished, Clopin, the gypsies' leader and master of ceremonies, announced that the King of the Festival of Fools was to be crowned.

As people in masks scrambled up onto the platform, Esmeralda spotted Quasimodo and pulled him up on stage, too. Then she went down the line of contestants, removing each mask as she went. When she came to Quasimodo, she realised that he wasn't wearing a mask at all!

There were gasps from the crowd but Clopin said, "We wanted the ugliest face in Paris. Here it is!"

Quasimodo was paraded through the streets as the ugliest King of Fools ever. However, the crowd soon began to tease Quasimodo and throw fruit at him. Then they tied him up. Frollo, who had been watching, sat back and did nothing, even when the frightened Quasimodo begged for his help.

25

It was Esmeralda who came to Quasimodo's rescue. Enraged, Frollo ordered the gypsy girl's arrest. In a mad chase she dodged the soldiers and with Djali slipped into the cathedral. Phoebus followed but, enchanted by Esmeralda, did not arrest her. When Frollo arrived, Phoebus told him that Esmeralda had claimed sanctuary – meaning she would be safe inside the cathedral.

Furious, Frollo and his guards left the cathedral.

From a hiding place, Quasimodo watched Esmeralda as she explored the cathedral. When Quasimodo realised that Esmeralda had seen him, he panicked and ran off to his room. Esmeralda followed Quasimodo, wanting to apologise for what had happened at the festival.

Up in the bell tower, Esmeralda spoke kindly to Quasimodo and praised his miniature city. As he talked with her, Quasimodo began to think that the bad things Frollo had said about the gypsies might not be true. And when Esmeralda told him he was not the monster his master said he was, Quasimodo desperately wanted to believe her.

30

Esmeralda was anxious to get back to her people but she knew Frollo's soldiers were waiting for her. Quasimodo offered Esmeralda a surprising way to escape. Picking up the gypsy and Djali, the bell ringer leapt off the bell tower and climbed down the side of the cathedral.

When they were safely on the ground, Esmeralda gave Quasimodo a woven necklace. "It will help you find the Court of Miracles," she said. Then she fled.

Back in the bell tower, the gargoyles told Quasimodo that they thought Esmeralda was in love with him.

"She can't be," said Quasimodo, but secretly he hoped it was true.

Frollo was furious when he learnt that Esmeralda had escaped and ordered his soldiers to search every building in Paris for her. In his rage he even set fire to the home of a miller, thinking he had sheltered gypsies.

Phoebus, now realising how truly evil Frollo was, bravely rescued the miller's family. Frollo immediately sentenced him to death. But Esmeralda, who had been hiding nearby, frightened Frollo's horse, and Phoebus tried to escape...

As he fled, Phoebus was wounded by an arrow, and fell, unconscious, into a river. Frollo left him for dead but Esmeralda rescued Phoebus and took him to Notre Dame.

At first Quasimodo thought Esmeralda *did* care deeply for him. But he soon realised that she had come only as a friend, wanting him to hide Phoebus. Quasimodo was heartbroken.

Suddenly, they heard Frollo approaching. Esmeralda turned to Quasimodo and asked him to protect Phoebus. As Esmeralda left, Quasimodo hid Phoebus under a table.

35

Frollo went straight to the bell tower. He noticed that Quasimodo was acting strangely, which made him suspicious. Then he spotted the little carved figure of Esmeralda that Quasimodo had added to his miniature city and a plan came to him.

"She will torment you no longer," Frollo assured Quasimodo. "I know where her hideout is and tomorrow at dawn, I will attack with a thousand men!"

As soon as Frollo left, Phoebus, now awake, asked Quasimodo to help him find Esmeralda. At first Quasimodo refused, afraid to disobey Frollo again. But he knew that the wounded Phoebus would not get far without his help. At last, thinking of his friendship with Esmeralda, he set out after the Captain. Frollo watched from the shadows.

The map on Esmeralda's necklace led the two men to the cemetery, where Quasimodo found a staircase hidden beneath the graves. The pair descended into the gloomy tunnels…

Suddenly, they were plunged into darkness. When the lights returned Phoebus and Quasimodo were surrounded by gypsies.

Clopin stepped forward. "Well, well, well," he said. "What have we here?" He had the two men gagged, and held a make-believe trial. Phoebus and Quasimodo were found guilty of spying for Frollo and sentenced to be hanged.

But Esmeralda burst through the crowd. "Stop!" she shouted. "These men are our friends!"

40

As soon as Esmeralda removed their gags, Phoebus
turned to the gypsies and warned them of Frollo's evil plans.

"You took a terrible risk coming here," said Esmeralda.
"It may not exactly show, but we're grateful."

"Don't thank me," Phoebus protested. "Thank Quasimodo.
Without his help I would never have found my way here."

"**N**or would I!" cried Frollo, triumphantly, arriving with his army. As the frightened gypsies tried to escape, Frollo walked up to where Phoebus, Esmeralda and Quasimodo stood.

"He led me right to you, my dear," Frollo said, sneering at Esmeralda.

"You must have tricked him!" accused Esmeralda.

The soldiers took Phoebus, Esmeralda and the other gypsies away, and Frollo gave orders for Quasimodo to be chained up in the bell tower.

44

By nightfall, a platform and stake had been set up in the square. As two guards tied Esmeralda to the stake, Frollo sentenced her to death.

Nearby, Phoebus was imprisoned in a cage surrounded by guards. He watched helplessly as Frollo approached Esmeralda.

In the bell tower, the gargoyles were urging Quasimodo to save his friend. But Quasimodo, defeated and in chains, remained motionless.

Then he heard Frollo's voice in the square below. "She stands before you," he boomed, "exposed for the monster that she is!"

"No!" cried Quasimodo, beginning to tug at his chains. He pulled with all his might and the pillars around him crumbled—he was free!

Quickly, Quasimodo swung down and rescued Esmeralda, who had fainted. Soldiers rushed at him, but he managed to hold them off.

As the crowd watched in amazement, Quasimodo carried Esmeralda up the face of Notre Dame. When he reached the balcony, Quasimodo raised the unconscious Esmeralda above his head.

"Sanctuary!" he cried. "Sanctuary! Sanctuary!"

"Seize the cathedral!" screamed Frollo, although he had no authority over the church.

Inside the bell tower, Quasimodo gently placed Esmeralda on a bed of straw. She was the one true human friend he had ever had and now he didn't know if she would ever wake up.

When Quasimodo walked onto the balcony, he saw Frollo's soldiers surrounding the cathedral. Suddenly, he was overcome with grief and anger.

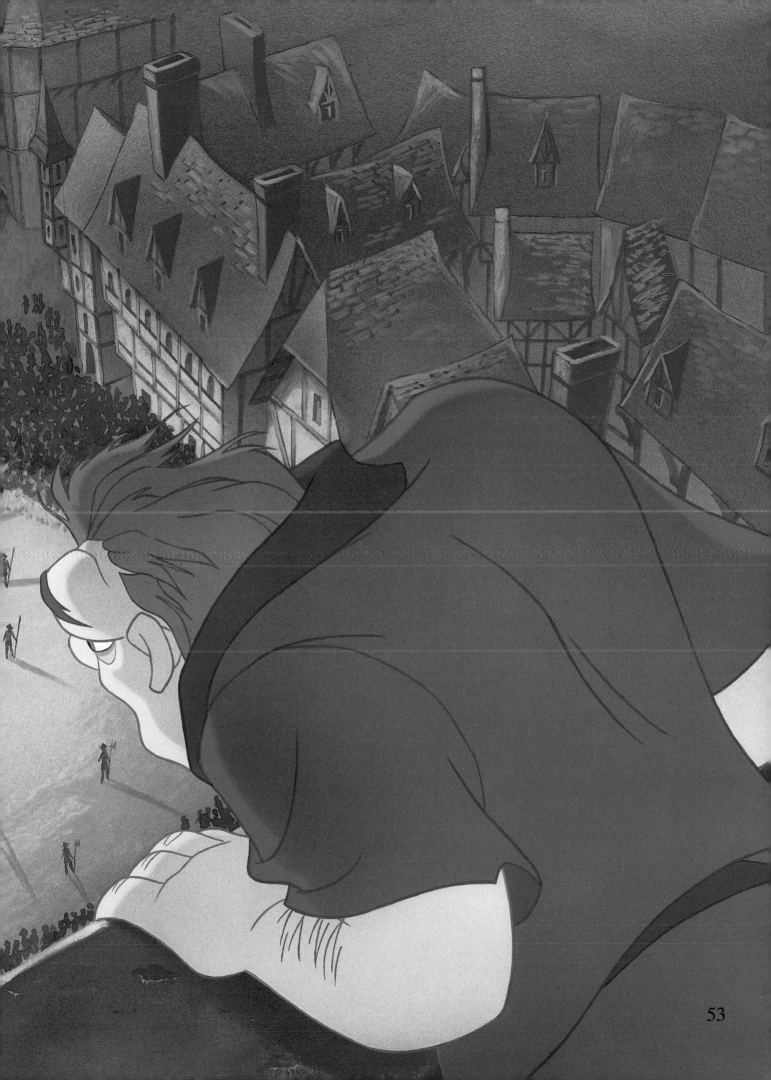

Meanwhile, Phoebus had seized the guard's keys and freed himself and Clopin from the cages where they had been imprisoned. He faced the crowd.

"Citizens of Paris," Phoebus cried, "Frollo has persecuted our people, ransacked our city… and now he has declared war on Notre Dame herself. Will we allow it?"

"No!" shouted the angry crowd, and Phoebus and Clopin led them towards the cathedral.

Inside Notre Dame, Quasimodo and his gargoyle friends were holding off Frollo's men in any way they could. But it seemed as if there was no end to the army and Quasimodo was getting tired. He could hear the doors of the cathedral giving way under the battering of the troops.

"It's hopeless," he muttered, stopping to rest.

Then he had an idea!

Hugo and Victor fanned the flames under a huge pot of lead that Quasimodo kept in the bell tower. Using all his strength, Quasimodo tipped the pot over. The glowing liquid flowed down over the wall and doors of the cathedral like a red-hot curtain.

The soldiers scattered, leaving Frollo alone in his rage.

Somehow, Frollo dodged the shower of lead and was able to open the cathedral door with his sword.

Quasimodo, however, didn't see him. When he looked out of the bell tower all he saw were the soldiers running away. "We've beaten them back!" he rejoiced. "Esmeralda, wake up! It's safe now!"

But Esmeralda continued to lie motionless on the bed of straw.

Soon Frollo reached the bell tower. He stood in the doorway, watching Quasimodo weep over Esmeralda's limp body.

"Is she dead?" Frollo asked, coming closer.

Quasimodo blocked his way. "You will not touch her!" he cried. "She was my friend!"

63

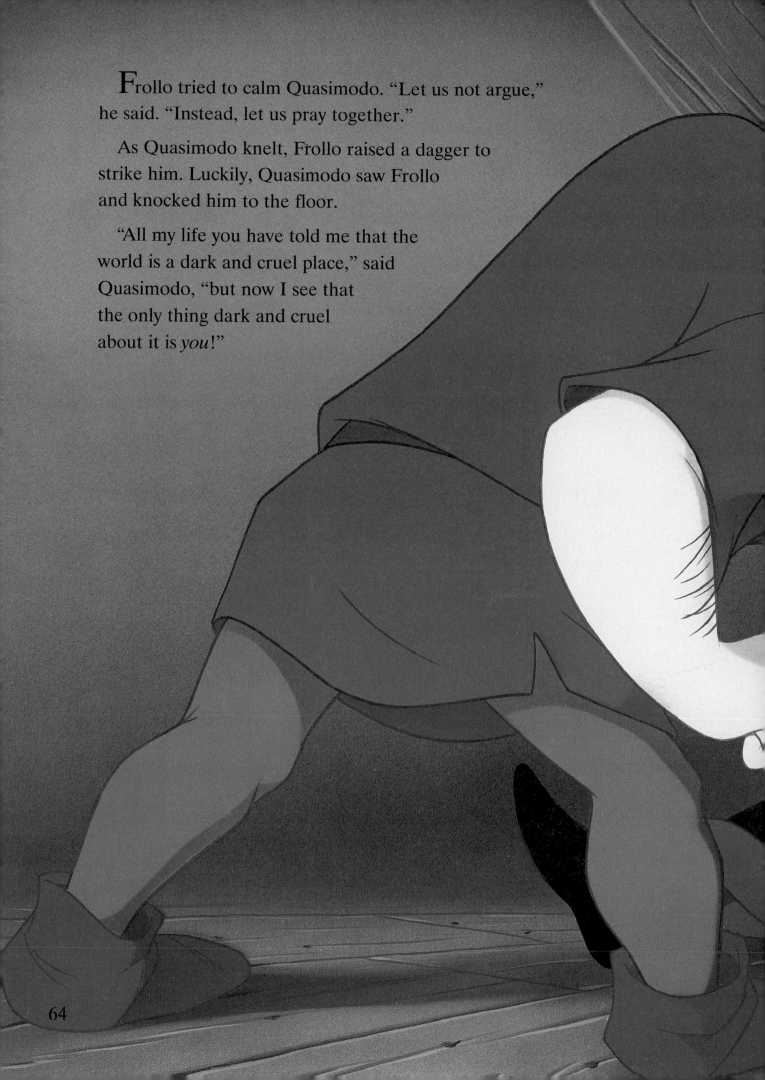

Frollo tried to calm Quasimodo. "Let us not argue," he said. "Instead, let us pray together."

As Quasimodo knelt, Frollo raised a dagger to strike him. Luckily, Quasimodo saw Frollo and knocked him to the floor.

"All my life you have told me that the world is a dark and cruel place," said Quasimodo, "but now I see that the only thing dark and cruel about it is *you*!"

Just then, a voice called softly, "Quasimodo."

It was Esmeralda! Quasimodo ran to her side and picked her up as Frollo, his sword drawn, pursued them onto the balcony. As Frollo lashed out at him, Quasimodo tried to hold on to Esmeralda. He managed to swing around the edge of the balcony, but Frollo kept attacking them.

At last, Quasimodo was able to carry Esmeralda to safety.
Then he climbed on top of a gargoyle and faced Frollo.

After a struggle, both Quasimodo and Frollo fell from the
balcony. Esmeralda managed to grab Quasimodo's hand,
while Frollo, at the last moment, climbed onto another
gargoyle.

With Esmeralda in striking distance, Frollo raised his sword. Just then, the gargoyle under him cracked and broke, sending Frollo plummeting to his death.

Esmeralda couldn't hold on to Quasimodo any longer. She lost her grip on his hand, and he, too began to fall.

Then, from a ledge below, Phoebus leaned out and caught their brave friend.

As morning dawned, the people of Paris gathered outside Notre Dame. When the cathedral doors opened, Esmeralda and Phoebus walked out into the square, hand in hand. A moment later, Esmeralda beckoned and Quasimodo emerged into the sunlight.

No one was sure what to say or do until a little girl walked up to Quasimodo. Gently, she reached up and touched his face.

"Three cheers for Quasimodo!" cried Clopin.

"Hip! Hip! Hooray!" shouted the jubilant crowd, as they carried Quasimodo on their shoulders through the square. He was truly the hero of the city and his face shone with joy.

High above, in the bell tower, Hugo, Victor and Laverne watched the happy scene. Finally, they could rejoice for their friend—he had found happiness at last.